# THE
# JUDITH KERR
## TREASURY

HarperCollins *Children's Books*

First published in hardback in Great Britain
by HarperCollins Children's Books in 2014

1 3 5 7 9 10 8 6 4 2

ISBN: 978-0-00-758653-0

Visit our website at www.harpercollins.co.uk

Printed and bound in China

# Contents

# The Tiger
# Who
# Came
# to Tea

*For Tacy and Matty*

Once there was a little girl called Sophie,
and she was having tea with her mummy
in the kitchen.
Suddenly there was a ring at the door.

Sophie's mummy said,
"I wonder who that can be.

It can't be the milkman
because he came this morning.

And it can't be the boy from the grocer
because this isn't the day he comes.

And it can't be Daddy
because he's got his key.

We'd better open the door and see."

Sophie opened the door, and there was a big, furry, stripy tiger. The tiger said, "Excuse me, but I'm very hungry. Do you think I could have tea with you?" Sophie's mummy said, "Of course, come in."

So the tiger came into the kitchen and sat down at the table.

Sophie's mummy said, "Would you like a sandwich?"
But the tiger didn't just take one sandwich.
He took all the sandwiches on the plate
and swallowed them in one big mouthful.
Owp!

And he still looked hungry,
so Sophie passed him the buns.

But again the tiger didn't eat just one bun.
He ate all the buns on the dish.
And then he ate all the biscuits
and all the cake,
until there was nothing
left to eat on the table.

So Sophie's mummy said,
"Would you like a drink?"
And the tiger drank
all the milk in the milk jug
and all the tea in the teapot.

And then he looked round the kitchen

to see what else he could find.

He ate all the supper
that was cooking in the saucepans…

…and all the food in the fridge,

…and all the packets and tins in the cupboard…

…and he drank all the milk,
and all the orange juice,
and all Daddy's beer,
and all the water in the tap.

Then he said,
"Thank you for my
nice tea. I think I'd
better go now."

And he went.

Sophie's mummy said, "I don't know what to do.
I've got nothing for Daddy's supper, the tiger has
eaten it all."

And Sophie found she couldn't have her bath
because the tiger had drunk all the water in the tap.

Just then Sophie's daddy came home.

So Sophie and her mummy told him what had happened, and how the tiger had eaten all the food and drunk all the drink.

And Sophie's daddy said, "I know what we'll do.
I've got a very good idea. We'll put on our coats
and go to a café."

So they went out in the dark, and all the street lamps were lit, and all the cars had their lights on, and they walked down the road to a café.

And they had a lovely supper with sausages and chips and ice cream.

In the morning
Sophie and her mummy
went shopping
and they bought
lots more things to eat.

And they also bought
a very big tin of
Tiger Food, in case
the tiger should
come to tea again.

But he never did.

# MOG
## the Forgetful Cat

*For our own Mog*

Mr Thomas

Mrs Thomas

Nicky

Debbie

Once there was a cat called Mog.
She lived with a family called Thomas.
Mog was nice but not very clever.
She didn't understand a lot of things.
A lot of other things she forgot.
She was a very forgetful cat.

Sometimes she ate her supper.
Then she forgot that she had
eaten it.

Sometimes she thought of something
in the middle of washing her leg.
Then she forgot to wash the rest of it.

Once she forgot
that cats can't fly.

But most of all she forgot her cat flap.
The cat flap led from the kitchen
into the garden.
Mog could go out…

…and in
again.
It was
her
own
little
door.

The garden always made Mog very excited.
She smelled all the smells.
She chased the birds.
She climbed the trees.
She ran round and round
with a big fluffed-up tail.
And then she forgot the cat flap.
She forgot that she had a cat flap.
She wanted to go back into the house,
but she couldn't remember how.

In the end she sat outside the kitchen window
and meowed until someone let her in.

Afterwards you could always tell
where she had sat.
This made Mr Thomas very sad.
He said, "Bother that cat!"
But Debbie said, "She's nice!"

Once Mog had a very bad day.
Even the start of the day was bad.
Mog was still asleep.
Then Nicky picked her up.
He hugged her
and said, "Nice kitty!"
Mog said nothing.
But she was not happy.

Then it was breakfast time.
Mog forgot that cats have milk for breakfast.
She forgot that cats only have eggs as a treat.

She ate an egg for her breakfast.
Mrs Thomas said, "Bother that cat!"
Debbie said, "Nicky doesn't like eggs anyway."

Mog looked through her cat flap.
It was raining in the garden.
Mog thought, "Perhaps the sun is shining in the street."
When the milkman came she ran out.
The milkman shut the door.

The sun was not shining in the street after all.

It was raining.

A big dog came down the street.

Mog ran.

The dog ran too.

Mog ran right round the house.
And the dog ran after her.
She climbed over the fence.
She ran through the garden
and jumped up outside the kitchen window.
She meowed a big meow,
very sudden and very loud.

Mrs Thomas said, "Bother that cat!"
Debbie said, "It wasn't her fault."

Mog was very sleepy.
She found a nice warm, soft place
and went to sleep.
She had a lovely dream.
Mog dreamed that she had wings.

She could fly everywhere.
She could fly faster than the birds,
even quite big birds…
Suddenly she woke up.

Mrs Thomas said, "Bother that cat!"
Debbie said, "I think you look nicer without a hat."

Debbie gave Mog her supper
and Mog ate it all up.
Then Debbie and Nicky went to bed.

Mog had a rest too,
but Mr Thomas wanted to see the fight.
Mr Thomas said, "Bother that cat!"

Mog thought, "Nobody likes me."
Then she thought, "Debbie likes me."
Debbie's door was open.

Debbie's bed was warm.
Debbie's hair was soft, like kitten fur.
Mog forgot that Debbie was not a kitten.

Debbie had a dream.
It was a bad dream.
It was a dream about a tiger.

The tiger wanted
to eat Debbie.
It was licking her hair.

Debbie shouted.
Mog jumped.
Mr and Mrs Thomas said,
"Bother, bother,
BOTHER that cat!"
Debbie said nothing.
She was still crying
because of the bad dream.

Mog ran out of the room
and right through the house
and out of her cat flap.
She was very sad.
The garden was dark.
The house was dark too.
Mog sat in the dark
and thought dark thoughts.
She thought, "Nobody likes me.
They've all gone to bed.
There's no one to let me in.
And they haven't even given me my supper."

Then she noticed something.
The house was not quite dark.
There was a little light moving about.
She looked through the window
and saw a man in the kitchen.
Mog thought, "Perhaps that man will let me in.
Perhaps he will give me my supper."

She meowed her biggest meow,
very sudden and very, very loud.
The man was surprised.
He dropped his bag.
It made a big noise
and everyone in the house woke up.

Mr Thomas ran down to the kitchen
and shouted, "A burglar!"
The burglar said, "Bother that cat!"
Mrs Thomas telephoned the police.
Debbie let Mog in
and Nicky hugged her.

A policeman came and they told him what had happened.
The policeman looked at Mog.
He said, "What a remarkable cat.

I've seen watch-dogs, but never a watch-cat.
She will get a medal."
Debbie said, "I think she'd rather have an egg."

Mog had a medal.

She also had an egg every day for breakfast.

Mr and Mrs Thomas told all their friends about her.

They said, "Mog is really remarkable."

And they never – (or almost never) – said, "Bother that cat!"

# One Night
# in the Zoo

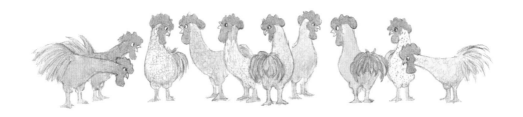

*For Ian Craig who made this book possible,*
*with love and thanks*

One magical, moonlit night in the zoo

An elephant jumped in the air and flew.
But nobody knew.

Then a crocodile and a kangaroo
Set off on a bicycle made for two,

And three lions did tricks which astonished a gnu.
But nobody knew.

Four bears cooked a squid and squidgeberry stew

Which turned five flamingos
from pink to blue.

Six rabbits climbed a giraffe for the view.
But nobody knew.

Seven tigers sneezed: Atchoo! Atchoo!
Atchoo! Atchoo! Atchoo! Atchoo!
ATCHOO! And their seven sneezes blew
The feathers off a cockatoo.

Eight monkeys stuck them back with glue.
But nobody knew.

Then in the sky a pinkish hue
Broke through the dark, and as it grew
Nine owls cried, "Woo! Terwitterwoo!
The night is fading! Quickly! Shoo!
Back in your cages, all of you!"

The sun got up. The keeper, too.
Ten cocks crowed, "Cockadoodledoo!
He's coming! Quick! He's almost due!"

The keeper and his trusty crew
Found all the animals back on view
(excepting only one or two).

"They look so tired," he said. "All through
 That moonlit night what *did* they do?"
 But nobody knew…

...except you!

And here they are again.

# The Other Goose

*For my dear grandson Alexander Dante with love*

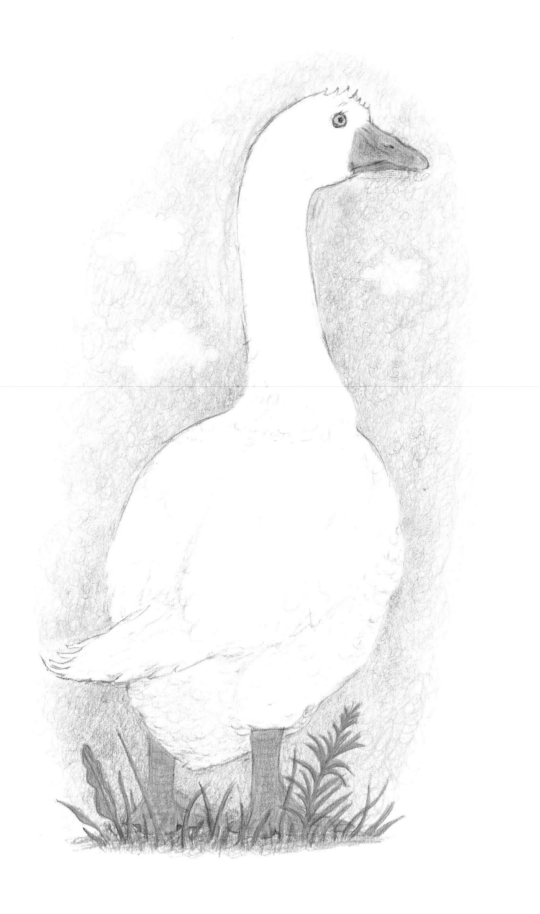

Once there was a goose called Katerina.

Katerina was the only goose on her pond.
There was no other goose.
This made Katerina very sad.

Sometimes Katerina thought she could see another goose.
She could see it in the side of a shiny car.
She stared and stared at it.
"One day that goose will come out," thought Katerina,
"Then I'll no longer be the only goose on the pond."

The shiny car belonged to Mr Buswell.
Mr Buswell looked after the bank across the road.
He said, "Just look at that silly bird.
Why do you keep staring at my car, Katerina?"

Katerina said, "Wakwakwak!"
Millie Buswell said nothing.
But she knew.

Everyone liked Katerina.
The baker liked her.

The lady from the toy shop liked her.

Miss Jones who taught dancing liked her,

and so did Bert from the fruit shop.
They all said hello to her on their way to the bank.

At the bank Mr Buswell looked after everyone's money.
"Take good care of it," said Bert.
Mr Buswell said, "Just look at that silly bird.
Have you come to help me take care of the money, Katerina?"

Katerina said, "Wakwakwak!"
Then she went back to stare at the shiny car.

But the other goose still wouldn't come out.

One day just before Christmas Millie Buswell said,
"We're all going to a party in the square, Katerina.
The mayor is going to switch on the Christmas lights."
Katerina said, "Wakwakwak!"
Then she tucked in her beak and went to sleep.

When she woke up it was dark and she was all alone.
She thought, "I'll go and see the goose in the shiny car."
But when she looked she had a big surprise.
The car was no longer shiny and the goose had gone.

It had come out. It had come out! It had come out at last!

"Now where is it?" thought Katerina.
It was not on the pond and not on the road.

Then she saw something. Something was moving in the dark.
"Wak!" she shouted happily. "Wakwakwak!"

But it was not
the other goose.
It was a man
with a bag.

It was a big bag.
It was a
goose-sized bag
and there was
something in it.

There was a
goose-sized thing
in that goose-sized bag.

Katerina shouted very loud, "Wakwakwak!! Wakwakwak!"
Then she flew at the man. She nipped his hand.
She tried to nip his nose.
The man shouted, "Get off!" and ran away.

But Katerina followed him

past the shops

and through the dark streets.

She shouted and flew and tried to nip.
She wished there was someone to help her.

In the square the mayor had switched on the lights.
Suddenly there was a lot of noise. It was the noise
of a goose shouting, "Wakwakwak!! Wakwakwak!"

"Just look at that silly bird," said Mr Buswell.
"Katerina, what are you doing to that poor man?"
Just then the man dropped his bag.

The other goose was not in it after all.
"Wak," said Katerina. She was very sad.
But everyone else was shouting.
"What's all this money?" shouted Mr Buswell.

"He's robbed the bank!"
shouted the mayor.

"He's robbed *us*!"
shouted Bert.
"That's our money!"

"But Katerina
stopped him,"
said Miss Jones.

"Oh Katerina," said Mr Buswell, "You have saved us all.
I will never, ever again call you a silly bird."

"This brave goose should have a reward," said the mayor.
"She shall have my best buns every day," said the baker.
"And my nicest fruit," said Bert.
"We could put up a statue to her," said Miss Jones.

"Good idea," said the mayor. "Anything else?"
Millie Buswell whispered in his ear.
"Really?" said the mayor. "Are you sure?"
Millie nodded. "All right then," said the mayor.

Next day the shiny car stopped right by Katerina's pond.
And then it happened. It really happened at last.
A goose came out of the side of the shiny car.
The mayor said, "Here you are, Katerina,
this is Charlie." And Millie said,
"He's going to live on the pond with you for ever."

Katerina and Charlie looked at each other.

Katerina and Charlie ate grass together.

Katerina and Charlie swam on the pond together,

and one day they made a nest together
and Katerina laid eggs in it.

And then there were not one, not two, not three, not four,

not five and not six, but seven geese on Katerina's pond.

"I always knew you'd come out of
that car in the end," said Katerina.

# When Willy Went to the Wedding

*For my husband Tom*

Once there was a boy called Willy.
He had lots of pets and a grown-up sister.
Willy's sister was so grown-up
that she was getting married,
and Willy was going to the wedding.
"Shall I bring my pets to the wedding?" said Willy.

"No," said Willy's father.

"No," said Willy's mother.

"No," said Willy's grown-up sister.

"Better not, old chap,"
said Bruce, who was
going to marry
Willy's sister.
"Your pets might
not like it."

So Willy did not bring his dog to the wedding.
He did not bring his cat or her three kittens.
He did not even bring his goldfish.
He only brought his hamster
because it liked to be in his pocket,
and his frog so that it would not be lonely.

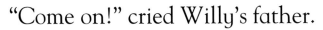

"Come on!" cried Willy's father.
"Everyone is waiting at the church."
It was not far.
"Remember to walk slowly,"
said Willy's father.
"And remember to
hold up my dress,"
said Willy's sister.

The church was full of friends and uncles and aunts.
They all turned to look at the bride.
"I think I'll take a picture of the wedding,"
said Willy's Uncle Fred.
Suddenly one of the aunts screamed.

"Look!" she cried.
It was not Willy's fault that his cat
had followed him to church.
It was not his fault that the three
kittens had followed the cat.

"Cats don't come to weddings," said the vicar.
Willy said, "I'll look after them."
The vicar gave them something to sit on.
Then he married Willy's sister to Bruce.

"Now for the wedding picture!"
cried Willy's Uncle Fred.
Everyone stood quite still.
But Uncle Fred did not stand still.
It was not Willy's fault that his
dog was waiting outside the church.
It was not his fault that the dog
was pleased to see him.

"How disgraceful!" screamed Willy's aunt.

"Take your pets home!" cried Willy's mother.

"At once!" cried Willy's father.

"I think they'd be happier there, old chap," said Bruce.

There was food and drink for everyone at home.
Willy said, "I'll give my pets something to eat."
The hamster was hungry too.

"Now I will take my picture of the wedding,"
said Uncle Fred.
But Willy's aunt screamed.
"A mouse!" she screamed.
"A horrible orange mouse!"

It was not Willy's fault that his hamster was hungry.
It was not his fault that the hamster liked cake.
And it was not Willy's fault that his frog wanted
a drink…

…or that his aunt was frightened of frogs…

…or that the cats got all upset.

None of it was his fault,
but everyone was cross.

"Take your pets away!"
cried his mother.
"Right away!"
cried his father.
"Away! Away! Away!"
screamed his aunt.

"But what about the picture?" said Willy.
"What about the picture of the wedding?
My pets should be in it.
After all they did come."

"No!" cried Willy's mother and Willy's father.
"No! No! No! No! No!" screamed Willy's aunt.
Uncle Fred set up his camera.
"I'd better go then," said Willy.
But Bruce said, "Stop!"
Willy stopped.
"I don't agree at all,"
said Bruce.
"I am very fond of pets
and I should love some
in my wedding picture."

"Just a moment!" said Willy.
He ran to get something.

Uncle Fred clicked his camera.
It was a lovely wedding picture.

"I'm glad my goldfish
wasn't left out," said Willy.
"Even a goldfish can enjoy
a wedding."

**Other bestselling books by Judith Kerr:**

## For Younger Readers:

## For Older Readers:

For readers of all ages:

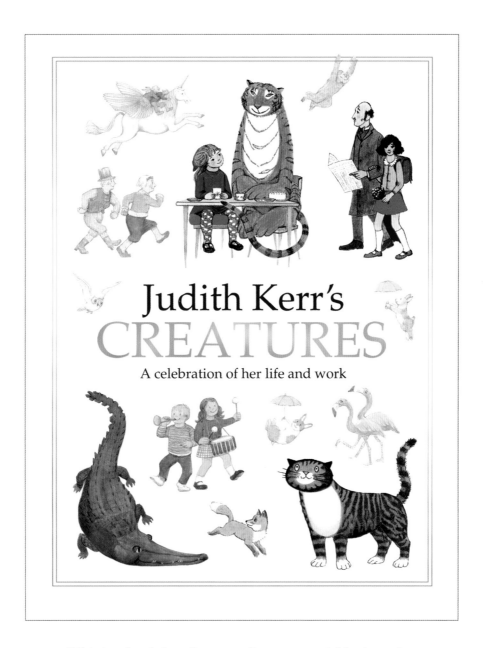

Judith Kerr's
CREATURES
A celebration of her life and work

"This is a book for all ages to linger over, richly deserving
to become another classic in its own right" *Independent*